DEVILS OF SERRA LYOA

SANAH J. D. MARA

A BOOK OF SHORT STORIES & POEMS

ISBN: 9798704409939

Cover Design by Mariatu Saccoh

Illustrations by Morrison Jusu, Mariatu Saccoh, and Sanah J.D. Mara

Maybe this is just a collection of myths. We have believed that the ancestors, and our local spirits are evil. That may not be the case for some. There's more to our culture than meets the eye. The essence of our ancestors are woven deep into our DNA. Things are not always what they seem. Real eyes realise real lies cloaked by a smokescreen of doubt. When the smoke clears, our vision becomes sharper than ever. Maybe then we can embrace the truth.

What makes a story real? Is every tale about the supernatural a lie, do spirits and demons exist? Or are they just a figment of our imagination? Is witchcraft real? If so, is it all evil? These questions plague us all. One thing I do know, is that if a story persists for so long, passing down from generation to generation, there has to be an element of truth in it. Other cultures in other countries have their tales of spirits and supernatural entities. It is my firm opinion that we have a right to explore our beliefs as well.

INTRODUCTION

Devils Of Serra Lyoa is a book of short stories and poems; that aim to shed light on the fascinating culture and local folk tales of Sierra Leone. Like other countries Sierra Leone has its own mythology or local folk lore about interesting characters, human, and spiritual. Sierra Leonean stories deserve to be brought to life, read, and appreciated worldwide. This book is for all ages of all nationalities in all settings. It is for all purposes: Whether read as a bed time story, a class room lesson, or leisurely. I hope readers get to experience culture, satisfaction, and get answers to elusive mysteries when they read this book. Sierra Leonean stories to the world!

....

Serra Lyoa is the Portuguese word for lion mountains, so named by Portuguese explorers around the fourteenth century, because the mountains resembled the shapes of lions, and the rumbling thunder during the rainy season sounded like the roar of a thousand lions. Over the years the name Serra Lyoa evolved to its modern-day permanent name, Sierra Leone.

ALSO BY THE AUTHOR

Thoughts From The Other Side - Poetry Book

Shortlisted for the 2020 Perito Prize

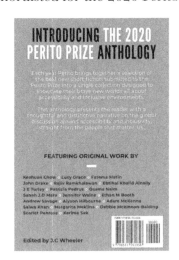

CONTENTS

PROLOGUE

"Do not be so quick to rejoice. Nature always balances extreme power. For every power, there is a bane. Harmony must be maintained. You can use the vanishing trick as much as you like for entertainment. However, you can only use it to gain wealth three times. Beyond that, you may lose everything altogether. Your grandpa knew this, yet he never used his powers to gain wealth. He was an honourable man. I belong to you now, and I will belong to your son and his sons, and their sons. Just obey my rules. Oh, and one last thing, be sure not to tell anyone about your gift. Humans are treacherous." Kuru says, his words echoing through my mind. I go to bed, my mind filled with thoughts of riches, things will soon change for the better.

...

A headless chicken lay with blood dripping from its neck
It still shuddered and moved with the little life left in it

A big black pot boiled on the fire, steam hissed and coiled upward
Loud chants rang through the hut

He held a knife in one hand, cowry shells in another
He rattled with one, slashed through the air with the other

He wore a red cloth wrapped around his waist
His head adorned with a brown cloth, his scarred chest naked

CHAPTER 1

D Juice Borbor En D Tire [1] (The Albino Boy and The Tire)

---

[1] The short story, The Albino Boy, was shortlisted for the International 2020 Perito Prize, and was published in the 2020 Perito Prize Anthology (In paperback & E-Book on amazon)

D Juice Borbor En D Tire (The Albino Boy and The Tire)

The children run around with nothing but rags around their waist. The dust rises beneath their feet, trailing behind them as they chase after one another. The object of their amusement is an old, busted, bicycle tire. One of the children controls it with a short stick. The tire rolls, wobbling from side to side, the children still chase it. Following it and giggling. The tire rolls into a group of chickens, which cluck and fly away as the tiny steps of the children thunder the earth. Their feet leave imprints in the dust.

Musa trails behind, the other kids do not like playing with him. He is different from them. He scratches his pale albino skin. Picks at the dark spots on his arms, and stares up at the bright blue sky. He brings his hand up to shade his eyes. He squints as the sun flares unforgivingly. He tries to compete with the sun and see how long he can gaze at it. He only lasts four seconds, before his eyelids burn and close involuntarily. He looks back down, wiping a tear from the corner of his eye. "Move! You are ruining the game!" One of the other boys says to him angrily. True enough, he has interrupted their game with his pause. Letting out a sigh, he chases behind them again, following the wobbling tire.

The tire continues spinning, with a trail of children behind it. Musa hits his toe on a tiny stone and falls forward into the child in front of him. Like a domino effect, the child in front of him bumps into the next child in front of him. It continues until the boy steering the tire, feels a bump at his back, and loses control of the tire. It rolls onto a patch of leaves, bumping into a rock at an awkward angle. The tire soars over a fence made of palm leaves and grass. The children hear it land with a thud, and quarrel over who should retrieve the tire. No one ever enters Pa Kambo's compound. Their parents had warned them that he was crazy. The entire village avoided him like a terrible plague. "Let Musa go and take it. He is a clumsy, stupid boy. If he does not bring it, we will show him pepper today!" One of the children says with a sneer. The kids then leave him behind and stomp away grudgingly.

Musa stands there scratching his blonde locks. As a blue-eyed albino, he is used to the harsh treatment. They call him names like *witch boy,* and the derogatory term [2]*juice borbor.* Only his mother treats him with kindness. To top it all off, he is an albino with dreadlocks. Talk about double trouble. He needs to retrieve the tire or else face the unforgivable beatings from his peers. There is a tiny opening in the fence, through which he pokes his small head through. He sees the tire lying on the ground, and tries to fit his lean frame through. He succeeds and makes his way towards the tire cautiously. He cannot help but marvel at the compound he is standing in. There is a tiny hut at one end. Lemon trees and rose apple trees grow in a clump together at another end. Little multi-coloured, birds play in the flowers surrounding the trees and chirp melodiously. He stares at the breathtaking sight, forgetting the tire.

He runs towards the tree of pink apples. They are far from reach. Luckily some have fallen on the ground. He picks one up, wipes it, and blows on it. He takes a bite and lets the sour-sweet white flesh crunch in his mouth. He sits down at the base of the tree, shuts his eyes and savours the fruity delight. He is too busy to notice that the brown cloth covering the hut has parted, and a figure is making its

---

[2] Juice Borbor - Local derogatory Sierra Leonean slang used to refer to an Albino

way towards him. He feels a shadow over him, opening his eyes, he spits out the fruit in his mouth with shock.

He stares up at the towering figure in front of him. The man's face is dark, with two long thin scars on either side of his face. His lean crooked arms show a hint of defined muscle uncommon for a man his age. The man adjusts his country cloth trousers while swatting a fly from his naked chest. He strokes his grey beard and scratches his bald head. Musa is very afraid, but the man smiles at him with crooked yellow teeth and sits down next to him. "Do not be afraid, here, have another apple." The man says to him gently. Still hesitant he accepts the apple from the man. The man's palms are coarse, with the flesh peeling off in some places. "Please call me Kambo, do not be afraid of me." Pa Kambo says to him. Musa nods his head, still unable to speak. "Can I tell you a story?" Pa Kambo asks. Musa nods once more. Pa Kambo stretches his feet, picks at his cracked toenails, and proceeds to talk.

"Have you ever heard of the [3]*Tamaboro?*" Pa Kambo asks. Musa shakes his head from side to side, meaning no. "The *Tamaboros* came from Koinadugu district in the Northern Province of Sierra Leone. *Tamaboros* were fearful Korankor hunters. *Tama* meaning lead and *boro* meaning bag. I will tell you about how Makuta Keita got her magic mirror. She was the most feared *Tamaboro* hunter. Yes boy, the *Tamaboros* had female fighters, they did not discriminate." Pa Kambo says, seeing the shock on Musa's face. Musa is not used

---

[3] Tamaboro - A group of Korankor hunters that played an integral part along with the Kamajors, Kapras, and Dunsos in the Sierra Leonean rebel war as vigilantes defending against the rebels.

to the idea of women being fighters. "To be a *Tamaboro*, one had to be initiated from an early age. *Tamaboros* were required to have a vast knowledge of all the bush paths, animals, and plants in the forest. After an initiate had proved themselves, they would then receive a special *ronko*. This *ronko* was brown, with black feathers, red cloths, and *sebe* attached to it. The successful initiate will then be bathed in a special, hot mixture until steam evaporated from his body. The mysterious preparation would make the newly initiated *Tamaboro* complete and invulnerable to even bullets." Pa Kambo continues saying, but pauses.

He places his rough hands in the soft hands of Musa's. They get up and walk across the grassy compound. They stop outside the hut and sit down on a long wooden bench by the brown, mud wall. A gentle breeze blows a piece of grass from the thatch roof to the floor. Musa holds a lemon in his other hand and offers it to Pa Kambo. The man smiles and peels the lemon, splits it in two, and gives the crescent-shaped fruit to him. He slips one in his mouth and looks up eagerly at Pa Kambo. Anxious for him to continue the story, no one besides his mama ever pays him this much attention. Pa Kambo picks his ears with his little finger and continues his story.

"It was initiation day, and Makuta Keita was to face Hassan Kama in the final competition. The winner would be part of the select few initiated that year. They had battled against each other for ten minutes. They were trading blow for blow. The fight seemed to have no end. Without warning, Makuta did something brilliant. She pretended to lie still on the floor like she had given up. Hassan moved in to strike the finishing blow. Cunningly Makuta grabbed his hand. She rolled away, pulled him towards her, and wrapped her leg around his head. She had one foot on his windpipe, and the other foot pinned to the back of his neck. The result was a deadly triangular chokehold. Hassan had no choice but to give up. The crowd cheered, amazed at the display of from Makuta. The cheering was interrupted by a shrill whistle. Everyone recognised the sound and ran away in fear. Sure enough, the creature appeared, showing only a hideous face with pointed ears. The rest of its body was a blur of whirlwind. The wind was angry and violent, blowing the thatch roofs from the huts. The trees bent over, stripped off their leaves. When the wind cleared, Makuta was gone." Pa Kambo says, stopping for a bit, catching his breath.

"A *ronsho* had captured Makuta. It was all the people talked about for the next three days. No one ever returned after being taken away by the wind devil. The *Tamaboros* decided to go along with the initiation. Hassan would take Makuta's place. The ceremony was almost at an end, and the witch doctor was about to place the fortified [4]*ronko* on Hassan. Suddenly he was interrupted by a sharp yell. Everyone gasped, it was Makuta. She stepped out of a whirlwind and took a bow in front of the other initiates. Hassan was cast to the side, while Makuta received her *ronko*. According to her, the *ronsho* carried her to its secret cave in the forest. However, it was impressed by the fact that she was not scared by it. Her bravery and intellect intrigued the creature. It was a creature that hated cowardice. From that day, the legend of Makuta was born. Makuta was

---

[4] Ronko - Traditional garment worn by hunters and warriors in Sierra Leone, that is said to usually be enchanted and fortified with mystical powers.

a fearsome warrior. You would see her every day in her *ronko*, staring back at her albino reflection in her enchanted mirror. The mirror was a gift from the [5]*ronsho*. With the mirror, she saw everything. With it, no enemy could hide from her. She could locate anyone, no matter the hiding place." Pa Kambo ends his story here while laughing at the look of surprise on Musa's face. Musa is amazed at what he has just heard! A legendary warrior, that was just like him! Maybe he has no reason to be ashamed. It is getting late now, he smiles at Pa Kambo and nods his head happily. "Will you tell me more stories next time?" He says to Pa Kambo. "Yes, you are welcome here anytime." Pa Kambo, replies. Musa rises from the bench, walks across the compound to where the tire lay. He picks it up, slides it across his shoulder, and crawls through the opening in the fence. He bends down and picks up a stick. Then slides it inside the tire, and starts spinning it. He can not wait to get home and tell his mama about the *Tamaboros*.

Pa Kambo is pleased. For the first time in a while, he has found companionship. He enters his hut, walking past a brown *ronko* with black feathers, red cloths, and [6]*sebe* attached to it, hanging on the wall. He smiles a nostalgic smile as he lays down on his grass bed. Meanwhile, a happy albino child with golden locks bouncing on his head runs along the dusty village path with a tire rolling in front of him.

---

[5] Ronsho - A whistling wind devil in local Sierra Leonean folklore, that is said to appear as a wind gust

[6] Sebe - Talisman to be worn around the elbows and knees of fighters, for protection and to ward of evil spirits. Also appears as a leather pouch attached to ronkos etc

CHAPTER 2

The Ronsho (The Wind Devil)

The Ronsho (The Wind Devil)

It was a dark starry night
The moon shone proud and bright
The crickets chirped, and other insects took flight

The trees cast ominous shadows in the dark
He walked down the road, each footstep leaving a mark
His eyes and ears alert for any surprise attack

He soon arrived at his destination
With outstretched hands, he chanted his manifestation
From behind the bush, two red spots made their way to him with determination

He had heard the stories, the tales of the wind devil
Being face to face with it now at eye level
A chill went up his spine as he stared at the creature in marvel

It was short, with ears so sharp they could slice the air in cuts
Its face twisted, with eyes appearing in the darkness as bright red dots
Most peculiar were its feet, its ankles faced forward, and its toes turned backward of sorts

It knew why he was there
He was wary of the surrounding air
According to fireside tales, its breath could leave your body with deep cuts that burned like fire

He kept his distance
It seemed more scared of him than he was of it, he took no chance

The Ronsho (The Wind Devil)

It stretched out its hands
He stretched open his palms
It dropped a small object in his hands
He watched as it did a little dance

He had got what he wanted
Their contract had started
There was only one way this story ended

Legend had it that the *ronsho* would grant you vast riches
As all things of the devil, there was a price for your wishes
In time it would eventually take away all your wealth, and leave all
your achievements in ashes

So as his new victim retreated, happy at the idea of wealth got
through slippery means
The *ronsho* let out a high pitched whistle and disappeared in a flurry
of winds
These humans never learned, greed was at the centre of their
hopes and dreams

CHAPTER 3

Sunday Morning Na Di Mami E Veranda (Sunday Morning On Granny's Porch)

Sunday Morning Na Di Mami E Veranda (Sunday Morning On Granny's Porch)

What a beautiful morning, the smell of the hibiscus flower drifts through the fresh, crisp air. Such an inviting fragrance. Birds and insects fly around in no particular direction, the cock crows as the gold rays of the sun filter through the pale blue sky. The sound of nature's orchestra conducted by the supreme being plays through the environment. I stare up, squinting as I try to count the wispy cotton clouds. "Ada steady your head!" She says to me in a very patient voice. "Sorry, granny," I reply ashamed. I am ashamed because she is so patient and gentle with me. I steady my head as I position my little plump body firmly between her knees. I let my hands caress her old legs. My fingers graze her protruding veins around her ankles. I try to feel every scar until I reach her knee and give it a gentle tap. I feel safe and secure between mama Adeola's knees. It is the most warm and inviting place in the world.

Her fingers move through my hair, slowly and steadily. She completes one braid, then parts with a dark brown comb and starts another. Her mother had used the same comb on her, and I will use it on my daughter one day. While she braids, she pauses to sip some warm ginger beer from a yellow glass beside her, I know she is about to tell me a story. She hands me a peppermint, first unwrapping the orange wrapper for me. I smile and joyously rattle the smooth candy around my mouth. Minty flavour explodes in my mouth as I listen to granny tell me a story of the dog and the cat, as she completes another braid.

"One night a witch visits a man, the witch leaps over the fence, and flies through the night sky on her broom to his window. Standing at

Sunday Morning Na Di Mami E Veranda (Sunday Morning On Granny's Porch)

the entrance is a dog. It barks at the witch and attacks it ferociously, telling it to go away. The witch flies away angrily. On another night, the witch flies to another house. Guarding the entrance is a black cat. The cat stares with its yellow eyes at the witch, purrs softly, and lets in the witch. The witch smiles a wicked smile and performs her enchantments around a sleeping man. She leaves out the window, with the cat perched on her broom, and they fly over the treetops towards the moon. So this is why in our society, the dog is our best friend, and people think cats are evil dear Ada." Granny says to me. "Are cats really evil?" I ask. Granny lets out a chuckle. She is done with my braids now, I bring my tiny hands to my head and pat my braids. I look up at granny, and we smile at each other. I never want these moments to end.

The moments did end. My granny passed away ten years ago in her sleep. I sit by my window on Sunday mornings, reminiscing about her calm voice and ginger beer breath. I miss her stories, and I miss her. Not even the humming of bees can cheer me up. A teardrop escapes my eye and rolls down my cheek. My heart aches as I long for the Sunday mornings on her porch. I can hear a soft meow, I turn around and hug my cat Adeola.

CHAPTER 4

Di Witch-Man Hunter (The Witch Hunter)

Di Witch-Man Hunter (The Witch Hunter)

The pitter-patter of raindrops drowns the night time noise
The tempo of their drops increase with each passing second

The downpour beats the earth
The water slaps the leaves and slides to the ground

Collecting in a puddle on the soft brown earth
His barefoot causes a tiny splash as he moves silently

Under the watchful eye of a crescent-shaped moon
He moves, moves with poise and purpose

He comes to a cluster of trees with the faint sound of chanting filtering through
With a cutlass in one hand, he hacks away at the leaves

Leaving an opening wide enough for him to look through
His neck itches, reaching a hand up to scratch it, he leans against a tree

He readjusts his brown waist-length gown
The gown is littered with amulets, specially prepared by an albino

He can see them now, they gather around a blue flame
Dressed in all black, some of them standing upside down

He can see the skulls of children in the middle
The scenery confirms his suspicions

Di Witch-Man Hunter (The Witch Hunter)

These are the witches that have been draining the blood of the village kids
He reaches into a brown bag slung around his shoulder

He pulls out a hollow tube wrapped with red cloth and cowries
Sticking his cutlass into the ground, he points the *witch gun* and takes aim

The bullets are invisible and dangerous only to evildoers
In seconds, it strikes a shrouded figure standing upside down

It lets out a blood-curdling scream causing the others to look around confused
Its too late, from the guise of his cover, his gown renders him invisible

He fires off more bullets, one by one the witches all crumble to the ground
Moving through the clearing, he beheads every one of them

The blue flame gets smaller and smaller till it extinguishes completely

He retreats for the night, exhausted, its been another successful witch hunt

CHAPTER 5

How Momoh E Poyo Sawa (How Momoh's Palm-Wine Went Sour)

How Momoh E Poyo Sawa (How Momoh's Palm-Wine Went Sour)

The sun was extra hot today, and its rays filtered through the palm tree beautifully. A brown lizard crawled across his foot, but he still maintained his poise. The lizard nodded its head up and down. It crawled across the red line marking the tree. He readjusted the elastic band holding him in place, attached to the tree. He wiped away beads of sweat across his forehead with the back of his hand. He only had to wait for a little bit more to claim his sweet reward. Mansu itself had picked out this tree for him. Ah, he could hear the last trickle roll into his brown gourd. That was his favourite part, hearing those final drops give a gentle splash, as they landed in his container. He stuck a cork into his gourd, slung it over his shoulder, and began the descent. Soon he was at the base of the tree and opened his container, he brought it to his dry lips and let a few drops slide down his tongue. It was his second favourite part. He gulped and licked his lips, the chief and the people would love this one. He had the sweetest palm wine in the whole village.

"Wow! Momoh! You have outdone yourself this time around." Chief Morlai said. He nodded, beaming with pride. His chief was satisfied with his tapping once again. He left the chief's hut, made his way along the grassy bush path, and headed home. He soon arrived, he parted the multicoloured cover and entered. He set down his large gourd on the ground and soon began pouring the palm wine into smaller containers. These he would sell to his customers. Everyone always wanted his wine. The other tappers in the village were jealous of his success. He wondered what his rivals would say when they found out that the chief had made him the official royal tapper. It was the most coveted title for a tapper in the village. All the tappers wanted the title, and now after years of perseverance, he had officially made it. He could not wait to see the looks on their faces at the next tapper gathering.

Evening soon reached, the sky had turned scarlet, he could see the black specks of birds flying across the sky. He walked past the river, the bag of cowries in the pocket of his brown khaki shorts rattled with each step. He peered behind his back, making sure that no one was following him. When he was sure no one followed him, he ducked into a large bush. He heard a twig snap in the background, on alert he looked around once more, but could see no one. It was probably just a figment of his imagination. The bush he had entered was enormous. Leaves grew in a circle around it, forming a natural enclosure. At the centre, grew a short palm tree. It was different from most palm trees. Its leaves were bright yellow, and its trunk lined with red streaks. He lay the bag of cowries at the base of the tree, and chanted "Mansu! Mansu! Mansu!"

Soon, he heard a loud hiss. From within the tree, moving over its yellow leaves was a gigantic white snake with red spots. It slid down the trunk of the tree and gracefully made its way towards him. He lay down flat on his face and kissed the ground. The snake moved over to him and hissed in his ear. Then it coiled its tail and circled the bag of cowries three times. It then opened its mouth wide, swallowed the bag whole, and slid up the tree once more. Soon it disappeared. Momoh got up from the floor and dusted himself. He smiled, Mansu had told him which tree he should tap next. Tomorrow he would find the tree marked with a red line. As long as Mansu got its cowries, and he was compliant, his Palm-Wine

How Momoh E Poyo Sawa (How Momoh's Palm-Wine Went Sour)

would always be the sweetest in the village. He made his way home but could swear he heard another twig snap behind him.

In the afternoon, after tapping the tree marked by Mansu, he made his way to the gathering of the other tappers. They were to meet at Sorie's hut. Here each of the tappers would exchange stories and taste each other's wine. He never drank anyone else's wine beside his. He had a good reason not to. His habit had become so notorious that the other tappers never bothered to offer him their wine anymore. They just gossiped behind his back, labelling him as proud. He wondered what they would say today. He was sure they had received news of his appointment by now.

On reaching Sorie's hut, everyone sat outside on long wooden benches. They were laughing and shaking each other's hands. Large gourds and wooden cups were on a small brown table in front of them. Everyone went silent when they saw him, then they burst into applause, cheering him loudly. Everyone besides Sorie, he made his way over to his fellow tappers and sat in the midst of them. Soon he was in deep conversation and laughter with his comrades. Surprisingly today, they had accommodated him, with no hushed whispers, just respect. He had earned their respect. The only one silent was Sorie, who strangely smiled at him. Today as per usual, he only drank from his gourd. Alas, soon, he was carried away by the potency of the wine and admiration from his peers. Drunk off wine and attention, he soon let his guard down.

Later the next day, on a warm, dry morning, Momoh made his way to the hidden bush by the river. He was light-hearted and hummed to himself while his cowries rattled in his pocket. Things were looking up, yesterday all his gourds sold out. Later in the afternoon, he would present fresh sweet palm wine to his chief, as the official royal tapper. On reaching the bush, he noticed something strange.

The leaves around it were withered and dark. They no longer formed a tight ring and were falling apart. Confused, he made his way through the bush. He panicked, the peculiar palm tree was different today. The leaves had changed colour from yellow to green, and the red streaks had disappeared from its trunk. "What is going on?" He asked out loud. He lay the bag of cowries at the base of the tree, and chanted "Mansu! Mansu! Mansu!" He repeated the chants ten times, but Mansu did not appear.

A dejected Momoh walked sluggishly along the dusty narrow bush path. His heart pumped fast and slammed against his chest wall with force. He wondered what to do now. He told himself to calm down. Mansu or no Mansu, he was a tapper, he would find any tree and tap it. So he came across a tall curvy palm tree, slung his gourd across his shoulder, secured the elastic band around him, and the tree. He began his ascent skilfully, soon reaching the top. He tapped the white nectar, slid down the tree, and brought the gourd to his lips for a taste. The drops of wine touched his tongue, but he spat them out with a cough, twisting his face in anguish. The wine tasted very, very, sour. He tried tapping three more trees but had no luck. All the wine he harvested tasted bad. Exhausted, he told himself that he was probably just sick, hence why the wine tasted different on his tongue.

How Momoh E Poyo Sawa (How Momoh's Palm-Wine Went Sour)

When he reached the chief's hut, he watched tongue-tied and scared as the chief tasted his wine. "Momoh! What is the meaning of this? I never want to drink your wine again!

I do not compromise!" The chief said, while coughing and spitting out the wine. Momoh felt like his life was over. His heart sank to the pits of his stomach. Scared and ashamed, he left the hut. He was perplexed. Walking along the bush path, he bumped into a blond-haired woman with light pale skin. The strange woman wore a white cloth with red spots on it. There was something eerie about this woman. She stood in one place swaying from side to side. Her movement was serpent-like. "Momoh, I warned you never to drink any other palm wine beside the one I showed you. You disobeyed me! You will never tap sweet palm wine again!" She said. A confused Momoh, moved forward to plead, but the woman vanished into thin air.

Momoh was furious. "When did I drink palm wine other than that which I tapped?" He asked out loud. The one golden rule from Mansu was that he was not to drink any other palm wine besides that which he tapped. He walked with his head bowed in thought until he bumped into someone. "I am sorry." He muttered. He looked up, smiling at him was Sorie. "Sorry Momoh, I heard the chief dismissed you as his royal tapper," Sorie said with a smile. Momoh stayed silent and let Sorie walk past him. "Momoh! One more thing." Sorie called out. He turned and faced Sorie again. "I followed you some days ago to your bush. I know your secret. At the gathering the other day, I switched your gourd with mine. Wish me luck. I start as the chief's new royal tapper tomorrow." Sorie

How Momoh E Poyo Sawa (How Momoh's Palm-Wine Went Sour)

said with a sly smile and walked away. Momoh stayed rooted to one spot while a shiver went through his body. He tried to form words, but could not. He just stood frozen in the middle of the path.

The days rolled by, no one ever bought Momoh's wine anymore. Banned from attending tapper gatherings, he spent his days at the base of palm trees searching for sweetness. Sweetness eluded him, avoided him, refused his pursuit. When asked why they never bought Momoh's wine, their answer was always the same: "Momoh's wine is never sweet, it is always sour." They would say this with a twist on their face.

CHAPTER 6

The Palm-Wine Tapper (The Brew Master)

The Palm-Wine Tapper (The Brew Master)

Turquoise blue skies filled with fluffy clouds
The wings of birds flap in reckless abandon
The sun shines through partially blocked by a cloud fluff

It's a calm day just like any other
Nature shows off its grand design
Flies buzz over fallen fruits

Hummingbirds and bees alike perch on flower petals
The monkeys swing from branch to branch
Dried leaves on the ground rustle and scatter

He takes his steps firmly and merrily
He moves with purpose and intention
Intensely he sets his sight on his target

How majestic she is, tall, slender, and curvy
She sways in the breeze, beckoning to him
He takes a bite off a red kola nut and slips the remaining piece in
his pocket

Savouring the bitter juice tickle his tongue, he cracks a smile
Cracks a smile with crooked teeth, stained brown by the kola nut
juice
He slings and ties a rope belt around her, double-checking the
tightness

The ascent starts, cautiously, and skilfully with a gourd tied around
his waist
He takes one step forward, slides the belt up further

The Palm-Wine Tapper (The Brew Master)

Takes another step forward, moves the rope up again
His steps elegantly marinated in repetition, and experience
In no time, he scales the graceful palm tree, his love

With precision, he cuts into the bark of the tree
Ties his gourd around the tree, allowing her sap to flow nonstop,
Flowing until it trickles

Emitting a potent scent that gently caresses his nose
His nostrils open wide to accommodate the familiar fragrance
After filling his gourd, he slides down with similar graceful fashion

Leaning his back gently against the tree, he tilts his head backward
Tilts and lifts his gourd, allowing the elixir to dribble into his
mouth
It glides on his tongue, sliding down into his throat

It moves like velvet, welcoming, soft and warm
He lets out a deep sigh of relief
Relishes the intoxicating taste of his labor,

There in the shade of his lady, he lay, embracing the life of a palm
wine tapper

CHAPTER 7

Okra Nor D Long Pas E Master (You Can Never Outgrow Your Elders)

Okra Nor D Long Pas E Master (You Can Never Outgrow Your Elders)

It was hot, dark, and stuffy. Pademba road prison had earned its name as the dungeon of despair, and rightfully so. As he stood, peering through the bars, he focused all attention on the tiny window in the wall. He gripped the bars with sweaty palms and banged his head on the metal. He scrunched up his nose at the smell. There were twenty of them sardined together in the cell. There was no hope for him, he slid down to the floor, careful not to step on someone. He sat there and thought about the events of last week.

He hated waiting for transport at the *Bottom Mango* roundabout. The lines were long, and the people sweaty. Today was no different, under the hot sun, the pavement radiated the heat, and it bounced from point to point, basking him in sweat. He slipped a white handkerchief from his pocket and glided it across his glistening forehead, then placed it back. How much longer did he have to wait? He pondered hailing an [7]*Okada* but decided against it no sooner the thought crossed his mind. The *okada* riders were reckless and raced the tarmac with no fear of injury or death itself.

A yellow taxi with blue, horizontal stripes braked in front of the queue. "Leicester junction! Leicester junction!" The young dark driver shouted. People ran at full speed towards the vehicle. He elbowed a young lady in a pink blouse, slid into the dusty, cracked leather seat of the car, and shut the door with a slam. Out of breath, he greeted the other passengers in the vehicle and handed a

---

[7] Okada: Local name for commercial motor bikes that transport passengers from point to point

wrinkled note of two thousand Leones to the driver. From the corner of the side-view mirror, the driver noticed a traffic police in a dark blue uniform and a light-reflective green jacket approaching. He sped off, for fear of having to bribe the officer with all his earnings for the day.

Amara sat and played with the cracked screen of his phone while looking out the window as they passed St. Mary's supermarket. The latest jams from Europe played from Capital Radio through the busted speakers of the taxi. They jolted over the bumpy road by *The Old School* entertainment complex. A local construction company won the bid to construct this Hill Station road. The result was uneven tar that felt like rowing a boat down a waterfall. As he sat there, he dreaded going home to his uncle. How was he going to explain it to him? That he had messed up at his job at Guarantee Trust Bank. His uncle had fought hard to get him that job. He hated how his uncle always talked down on him and advised him like he was a child. He never listened to his uncle's ramblings anyway. For him, money was the motivation, and he knew his uncle would change his mind when he told him about the money he had acquired.

He soon reached his uncle's Leicester home. The taxi dropped him off after the roundabout at Leicester junction. After a short walk, he arrived and tapped his knuckles on the black gate. He hated how long Pa Amadu the gateman took to open the gate always.

Okra Nor D Long Pas E Master (You Can Never Outgrow Your Elders)

He increased the tempo of his knock. The gate swung open, and his uncle stood there looking down at him angrily. He no doubt had heard of his dismissal from the bank. His only option now was to explain to him how he had diverted some funds illegally from a wealthy company, into an untraceable account that belonged to a friend. He was not going to let his uncle talk to him in any manner. He was a big man now, set for life. Uncle Samura opened his mouth to talk.

"Be quiet uncle!" He yelled at him. Uncle Samura was taken aback by shock and was about to no doubt unleash fury at him when their altercation was interrupted by the blaring horns of a black vehicle. The initials on the car number plate read CID 002. Two tall men in plain white clothes, one officer in blue camouflage uniform, and a red beret hopped out the vehicle. They were from the Criminal Investigations Department. "Amara, you are under arrest for money laundering and digital theft." One of the men said to him. His heart stopped beating, and his mind went dark. While being stuffed into the back of the car, he stole an embarrassed look at his Uncle Samura's stoic face. His uncle turned around and shut his gate. Distraught, he thought back to his uncle's advice a few months earlier: "Keep your head down nephew, go placidly amidst the tides of life, do not rush, and respect your elders. [8]*Okra nor d long pas e master.*" The Okra fruit no matter how long it grows does not outgrow its parent fruit.

---

[8] Okra nor d long pas e master: The Okra fruit no matter how long it grows does not outgrow its parent fruit.

Okra Nor D Long Pas E Master (You Can Never Outgrow Your Elders)

Now a week later, he regretted everything. He disclosed his dealings to the investigators and received a sentence of ten years by the judge.

He tried to get up from the floor to stretch his legs, while doing so, he felt a sharp slap at the back of his head. He had stepped on someone.

CHAPTER 8

The *Matorma* (The Masquerade Devil)

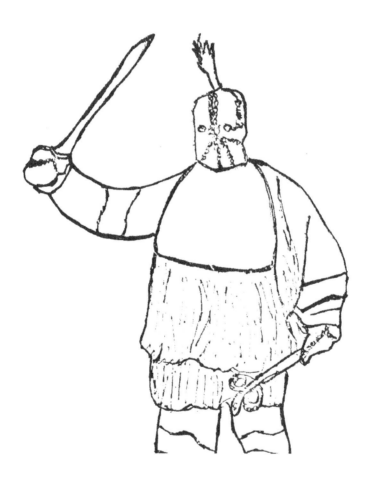

The *Matorma* (The Masquerade Devil)

The drums beat and the beads rattle
They dance in unison, their raffia skirts flying around
Its almost time for the harvest
The witches give them no peace

In a season of abundance
The witches come out at night to spoil their crops
The witches wreck the fruits of their labor
They have had enough, so they dance

They sing and dance
They sound the drums and manifest for it to come
Come it does, sword in one hand, cow tail whip in another
It comes out dancing and jumping in all its glory

Its head of red cloth, covered with white [9]*jege*
It twists and moves to the rhythm of the drums
Then it bends down and takes a knee on the dusty ground
The music stops, everyone kneels too

Only the cursed and forsaken stand when it kneels
It only pursues the wicked, always protects the innocent
It stands up and moves around the farmland
Music resumes in the background

Its red cloth signals the witches that danger is imminent
Its raffia skirt makes it appear larger than life

---

[9] Jege - cowries (these are believed to have mystical powers)

41

The *Matorma* (The Masquerade Devil)

With a swing of its sword, it is now in an invincible battle
It swings and twists, clashing with evil

With a final blow, a cloud of white smoke appears
When it clears, a figure dressed in black lies unmoving on the
ground
The *Matorma* dances over the captured witch
Its *jege*, blind and mesmerise the witch

The people celebrate and chant its name
Their devil has protected them once more
They now dance and jump, they will have a successful harvest
The *matorma* exits as the drums beat, and the beads rattle

CHAPTER 9

Di Cotton Tik Wae D Cry Blood (The Cotton Tree That Sheds Tears Of Blood)

Di Cotton Tik Wae D Cry Blood (The Cotton Tree That Sheds Tears Of Blood)

The bat flew from where it hung upside down on a large branch. Something had disturbed it. The other bats followed suit, and soon there was a large black cloud of bats soaring above the tree. Kanu was tired of running from the witch hunter and needed to disappear. He was almost home now. He placed his hand on the trunk of the tree and muttered an incantation out loud. He shrunk down in size and disappeared into the tree. He looked at the vast city in front of him, a witch in a [10]*granat canda* drove past him with speed. He lost his bearing for a moment but sighed with relief. He was home now, the magical city of Demabu at the heart of the cotton tree was a safe haven.

Demabu was grand and beautiful. Little black houses with no roofs, just walls, littered the streets. They housed the witches and wizards that dwelled in the city. There were narrow grey streets, paved with a shimmering material. Usually, there would be traffic of *granat canda* causing a jam. It was more pronounced in the evening when the workers left the magical potions factory. The leaves of the cotton tree acted as one big roof, only little needle-like rays of sunlight penetrated. Hence, it was always dark in the city, even during the day. To avoid traffic, some of the inhabitants flew around on brooms. Others, the night riders of the great witch Halija, flew around on big black bats. The most peculiar thing about this city was the red lines running from every house to the palace. The lines shimmered while red liquid flowed through them.

---

[10] Granat Canda - the shell of the ground nut, rumoured to be used by witches as a vehicle

Di Cotton Tik Wae D Cry Blood (The Cotton Tree That Sheds Tears Of Blood)

They shared a link with and supplied energy to Halija's palace, at the same time drawing essence from it.

Kanu placed his hand in his leather bag. His fingers touched something cold and wet. He smiled, Halija would be pleased. He had gone through a lot of trouble to secure these. It was almost the end of the year. The ceremony was to be performed just on the dot of the New Year. The stupid witch hunter almost ruined his plans, but he had prevailed. He made his way to the dark palace. Its entrance lined with black flowers while winged creatures, fairies flew around protecting it. He entered by placing his hand on the black wall, and muttering an incantation out loud. As with all houses in Demabu, there were no doors on the entrances. Only a true inhabitant of the magical city could enter into a Demabu residence. His body meshed with the black wall, and he soon appeared inside.

Halija wore black robes, as black as the most starless night, on the highest mountain. Not even her face showed, her entire being was darkness. She sat on a throne of bones and tapped on her throne with long bony fingers. There was a rule, no one spoke to Halija, if not a member of her council of elders. Kanu approached the throne steadily. He scratched his pointed ears and spilled the contents of the bag on the floor. The object was cold and sticky but glowed brightly. He brought up his hands to his eyes for shade from the glaring glow. Halija dismissed him with a wave of her hand. He made his way outside, his mission was complete, he was one step closer to being a night rider, and riding on a bat. He had just supplied Halija with a special cloth. In society, some children at birth were born with a glowing shroud wrapped around them. Kids with this shroud would grow to have great destinies. The city of Demabu thrived on two things; blood and stolen hopes. Now he had provided Halija with this golden shroud. The ceremony would be a success on New Year's Eve.

The moon shone in the night sky, only bits of its light managed to penetrate through the thick leaves. All the inhabitants of Demabu stood outside the dark place. It was almost time for the renewal ceremony, Halija appeared in front of the palace in the company of three other hooded figures. Together they were the four elders. They placed the glowing shroud on the ground, surrounded by blood they had harvested from children. Joining hands, they formed a circle around it and whistled in synchrony. They swayed back and forth, the red veins leading to the palace glowed bright red until a blue light emitted from the circle and penetrated the sky. It seemed to enter every leaf of the tree, basking it in a blue hue. The citizens of Demabu cheered. The renewal was a success. The veins connecting the houses to the palace now glowed blue. The magic of the city would continue to flow for the rest of the year.

After the success of the renewal ceremony, Kanu was now a night rider. Apparently, he had made a great impression on Halija. The next night he joined the others on a great black bat and flew outside of the city to hunt for more children. He glanced at the majestic cotton tree in all its glory. The massive trunk of the tree was bleeding. Scarlet blood dripped down like tears. It always happened once a year on New Year's Eve. The renewal ceremony would purge the city of the leftover blood of innocent souls.

Di Cotton Tik Wae D Cry Blood (The Cotton Tree That Sheds Tears Of Blood)

The purging ensured that magic flowed and charged the city and its inhabitants. As a result, the tree would shed tears of blood once every year.

CHAPTER 10

Di Ju-ju Man (The Voodoo Priest)

Di Ju-ju Man (The Voodoo Priest)

Thunder cracked, lightning flashed
The clouds parted, and rain poured through

Tiny drops dripped through the thatch roof,
Dripped and collected in a tiny pool on the floor.

A headless chicken lay with blood dripping from its neck
It still shuddered and moved with the little life left in it

A big black pot boiled on the fire, steam hissed and coiled upward
Loud chants rang through the hut

He held a knife in one hand, cowry shells in another
He rattled with one, slashed through the air with the other

He wore a red cloth wrapped around his waist
His head adorned with a brown cloth, his scarred chest naked

By his side on the floor, lay his patient
She had been sick for weeks, bones visibly showing

With each chant and rattle, her body jerked on the floor.
The chants got louder, the ju-ju man's body swayed and trembled

The spirits of the thirty-six devils he spoke to, flowed through him
They guided him, filling his head with the knowledge of healing

At the peak of the chanting, the thunder cracked louder
For a moment the *ju-ju* man went as still as a statue

Di Ju-ju Man (The Voodoo Priest)

The headless chicken rose from the floor
It rose while walking from side to side in a drunken gait

What a sight to behold, at the same time the patient jerked and got
up
The headless chicken on its feet, the sick patient on her feet

The *ju-ju* man had done it again, his devils had not disappointed
him
He grabbed the chicken and tossed it into the pot, a fitting sacrifice

The pot hissed one final time, the rain stopped
The *ju-ju* man gave his patient a potion to drink and bade her
farewell

CHAPTER 11

Tamba En D Kofo (Tamba and The Vanishing Spirit)

Tamba En D Kofo (Tamba and The Vanishing Spirit)

The rain beats the roof, letting out a metallic rhythm. Hill Station is always cold and foggy, but the wealthiest people of the land live up here. The night is extra dark and extra chilly. On tiptoes, we try to scale the wall of the mansion. The wall is smooth, except for a block of concrete in the middle. It is on this block we place our feet, climbing skilfully and steadily. We reach the top of the fence, which is protected by rusty barbed wire and sharp broken bottles. I can still hear the rain beating the roof. It is the perfect night for this job. We remove our thick raincoats, and lay them on the barbed wire, carefully and quickly we crush the covering with our boots, and jump over. Just before we land on the floor, we roll to cushion the blow.

I survey the compound we are standing in. It has a security post to the corner of the gate, with no dogs in sight. There is only one night-guard, snoring while a radio hums in the background. Two cars covered with dark cloths are parked just outside the mansion. This operation is going to be easy. I look at Peter, and he smiles back, we creep towards the front door, under the pouring rain. Peter tests the front handle, but it does not budge. I remove a thin wire with a hook attached at the end, from my pocket. I slide this into the keyhole, listening for a tiny click, the click comes, and I twist. Peter turns the lock, and the door opens. We are inside.

Inside the house is dark, we chose this house because the owner was a wealthy politician, and he was out of town for now. According to the information we received, he only left his old female care-taker behind to look after the premises. Peter feels around on the wall until he finds a switch and flips it on. The light floods the house.

Tamba En D Kofo (Tamba and The Vanishing Spirit)

We go past the living room and head up the stairs, not paying attention to our surroundings. What we have come for is upstairs in the master bedroom. According to our information, the master bedroom would be next to a tiny living room on the second floor. Sure enough, we find it and turn the handle. The handle turns, and the door opens. I switch on the light and see the most spacious room on which I have ever set my eyes. Peter brushes past me with his lean frame. He runs towards the massive bed excitedly, he spots the left bedside drawer and empties the contents. Happy, we fill our pockets with watches and bundles of cash. They will sell for a handsome price. Donald will be pleased.

Satisfied, we make our way towards the front door quietly. "Thief! Thief! Thief!" Someone yells out loud. An old lady in a white nightgown blocks the entrance while yelling frantically. Peter advances on her, chokes her throat, and holds a knife to her face. The lady whimpers, trembling with fear. "Be quiet, or I will cut your throat," Peter whispers. She reluctantly obeys. "Come with us and open the gate mama, we would not harm you," I say to her gently. I feel guilty on the inside, staring at her scared face. She is old enough to be my grandma. We follow the old lady under the rain while Peter holds a knife at her back. The security guard Is still sleeping, indifferent to the activities happening around him. I go inside and give him a hard slap on his face. He gets up shocked and angry, but on seeing a blade held at the back of the old lady, he calms down. There is an apologetic look on his face. "Open the gate, my man," Peter says. The guard hurriedly opens the gate, and we pass through.

"Thief! Thief!" The old lady yells to alert the neighbours. Peter tosses her to the ground, and we run towards our [11]*Okada*. The guard chases after us, and some lights start to come on in the surrounding houses. Our operation driver John has the engine revving already. We hop on the *Okada*, gripping each other tightly, and John speeds away. We avoid going to Regent because there will be a police checkpoint blocking the road by this time. Instead, John takes us to the back of [12]*Old School*. We arrive there, wet, cold, but safe. We hide in an unfinished building, tomorrow we will plan, now we rest. I sit up against the wall and think to myself how many more robberies do I have to do before I can afford to attend college.

I wake up with a stretch and rub my eyes. It is morning, and I can hear the chatter of children heading to school, and women with loads on their head discussing where they will hawk their wares. Peter lays flat on his face, with his hands facing upward by his side. I can see his green, spider-web tattoo on his lower left hand. I was there when he got it, but for fear of pain, I had thought against getting one too. I nudge him with my foot to wake him up. He gets up grudgingly, muttering a string of incomprehensible curse words. I look around for John, I do not see him, but he soon arrives with a black plastic bag containing three [13]*tapalapa* bread with sweet milk

---

[11] Okada: Local name for commercial motor bikes that transport passengers from point to point

[12] Old School: Popular entertainment gaming complex at Hill Station, Freetown, Sierra Leone

[13] Tapalapa: Very long locally baked bread in Sierra Leone

and three plastic sachets of water. We eat hungrily, hop on the *Oka-da*, and head towards Regent.

Donald's camp is massive, located at the back of Regent, behind a hill. It is a large compound of [14]*pan body* houses, with the metal carcasses of scrapped cars scattered around. Young boys and girls are moving around with gadgets in their hands. Almost every robbery that happens in the wealthy neighbourhoods of the city leads back to Donald. There is an unspoken rule of seven. Objects stolen are only held for seven days. If within the seven days an alarm is raised, the objects get returned to the authorities. After the seven days, if there is no alarm, then the objects can be kept. Donald was the master keeper, and he had deals with the police. So everyone came to him to store their stolen goods, and he did so in exchange for a percentage of the spoils, while at the same time offering protection.

We make our way to his house, the largest *pan body* of the lot. John parks, and leans his bike against the fence, he will wait for us. Donald is outside already, sitting down bare-chested on a wooden bench. He is locked in conversation with someone, but smiles when he sees us, and beckons us over. "Boys! I take it last night went well?" Donald says. We nod our head and spill the contents of our pockets gently into his large open palms. Donald eyes the items greedily and picks at his gold tooth with a toothpick. "Paul, here this is your cut," Donald says to the skinny boy next to him. "Peter

---

14 Pan Body: Locally built houses made up of zinc material

and Tamba, this boy here is the houseboy of the house you went to last night." Donald continues saying to us. Now we understand where the information came from yesterday. Donald had people like this all over. Informants, backstabbers, it did not matter who it was. If there was valuable information to be had, Donald always got it.

He places a bundle in Paul's hands, and the skinny boy leaves excitedly. Donald gives Peter and I a wad of one million Leones. We split it fifty-fifty and pocket it. He promises to contact us again if he hears something new. We leave his compound but overhear from the others that a thief had been caught at Leicester at five a.m this morning. He had been beaten, stripped naked, his arms and legs bound with wire, and a lemon shoved up his backside. We wince as we hear the story. We knew the young man. Being a thief had its rewards, but when caught, people were very unforgiving. We give John a bundle of green notes for his troubles. He pockets it in his faded blazer, swings on his *Okada*, and speeds off. "Take care of yourself Tamba, keep in touch," Peter says. I give him a fist bump and watch him leave, no doubt heading to a bar to enjoy his spoils. I cannot participate. I have more pressing responsibilities to handle.

I walk along the Regent road, heading down past a curvy hill until I reach the police station at the start of Bathurst junction. The police station still looks the same as it was during colonial times, its yellow and blue paint peeling off in some places. I advance up a hill opposite the station, walk a few more meters until I am outside a red *pan body*. A lady stands at the entrance with swollen red eyes, shaking her hands. She sees me and runs forward to hug me.

Tamba En D Kofo (Tamba and The Vanishing Spirit)

"Tamba! Tamba! He does not have much time. I have tried everything. He has been calling for you." Sister Binty says to me. I run inside, heart pounding, I make my way to his room, and barge in. He lays on the bed frail as ever, his breathing laboured. "Tamba? Come forward, boy." Grandpa Ali says weakly.

I step forward gingerly into the dimly lit room, the only source of light being the light rays that filter through the half-opened window. I spot a small piece of yellow paper with a pen next to it on the bedside table. I wonder what grandpa has been writing. The low hum of a standing fan turning from side to side sounds alongside his forced breaths. He is covered with a white cotton cloth, while a makeshift drip trickles liquid at intervals into his bulging veins. I hate seeing him like this. Usually, I always run to his room when I am stressed, sit by his foot, and converse with him. Today is different. I hold his hands, he gives my palms a feeble squeeze, and with great effort lifts his head some inches to talk to me. "My boy, I do not have much time, I know I have not been able to give you much, but I present a gift to you. You must only use it three times to get that which you want. Not more than three." Grandpa says. I am puzzled. What does he mean? I wonder to myself.

He grips my hand one last time, mutters a string of words that I cannot quite understand. The room goes very dark, the windows rattle violently, a cloud of smoke trails from his mouth, and gathers in the middle of the room. From the smoke, a man steps out. He is dark-skinned, covered with white paint markings, and a black cloth drapes around his shoulders. As if things could not get even more strange, his left-hand holds up a black skull permanently to the top of his head. His body seems to fade intermittently, appearing and

57

disappearing. I stare awestruck, not knowing what to make of this. Then he vanishes into smoke again, the smoke coils through the room like a serpent, it enters my mouth, my body shakes violently, my eyes darken, everything fades into blackness. Just before the darkness arrives, I can hear muffled words as if grandpa is trying to tell me something else.

I feel a splash of cold water on my face, and bring my hands to wipe my eyes, I am lying flat on the floor. I sit up hurriedly and stare into the anxious face of Sister Binty. "Tamba you passed out, I had to throw water on your face!" She says to me. I glance over to the body of grandpa, who is no longer breathing. I sigh loudly. He had raised me himself all these years after my parents had died in an accident on my fifth birthday. My grandpa was my rock, the only family I knew. Old age had not been kind to him, and now he was gone. "Sister Binty, be strong, we have to bury him, he would not want us to be disheartened," I say while tapping her shoulders to comfort her. Like me, she is a testimony of his kind heart. She was a struggling nurse in Freetown who was in dire need of a place to stay. Grandpa had offered her shelter for free. In exchange, all she had to do was look after him.

I leave her and head to my room. It is a small room, but I keep everything organised. Shoes in one corner, bed well made, and books arranged neatly on a tiny study table. I draw the faded, yellow window blind, to let some light filter through, I kneel by my bed and draw out a wooden box from underneath it. Carefully I open it and place some of the money Donald had given me, the balance I will use for grandpa's funeral. It is in this box I keep all my money, someday I will have enough for my college tuition. I lay my head on the bed, bring out my battered Samsung phone, and flick my finger across the cracked screen. "Tamba, is it? Why so sad? I will make you rich! Just do as I say." A voice says to me. I turn around fervently, looking around to see who is speaking. A cold shiver goes through my body. I cough, a trail of smoke leaves my mouth and gathers in the middle of the room. A figure steps from the smoke.

It is the same figure I had seen in my grandpa's room earlier. The hooded spirit, holding a black skull to its head. He levitates a few inches off the floor and floats towards me. "Do not fear. My name is Kuru the *Kofo.*" He says to me, his lips do not move, but I can hear him in my head. "What is a *Kofo*?" I ask, wondering what this has to do with me. "My boy, we are as old as time itself. We are spirits originated from the [15]*Loko* tribe. We used to have plenty of powers, but over time due to modernisation and occupation of our natural lands, these powers are now diminished." He continues talking to me in my mind. "So what can you do for me? How am I connected to all this?" I ask, this time not out loud, but in my head. The *Kofo* evaporates into smoke and floats towards me, the smoke enters my nostrils, filling my body, I feel the chill in my body, but this time not as overwhelming as before. It feels familiar.

"Let me show you what you can do. Go to the wall, place your hand on it, call out *Kofo* three times." He says to me. Puzzled, I move to the wall and place my hand on it.

---

[15] Loko: One of the tribes from the Northern Province of Sierra Leone

Tamba En D Kofo (Tamba and The Vanishing Spirit)

"*Kofo, Kofo, Kofo*," I whisper gingerly. My hand moves through the wall. I can feel my fingers wiggle free at the other end. Then my body follows until I am completely through to the other side. I can see the short hallway that leads to the living room. Mind boggled, I place my hand on the wall again and try to go into my room. I hit my head on the wall, wincing in pain. I wonder what is wrong. It had worked just a few moments earlier. Ah, I am such a fool, I place my hand on the wall again, and say "*Kofo, Kofo, Kofo*." Sure enough, my arm passes through, followed by my body. The sensation when my body passes through the wall is weird. I cannot feel anything. I just pass through silently. I smile, punching the air with excitement.

"Do not be so quick to rejoice. Nature always balances extreme power. For every power, there is a bane. Harmony must be maintained. You can use the vanishing trick as much as you like for entertainment. However, you can only use it to gain wealth three times. Beyond that, you may lose everything altogether. Your grandpa knew this, yet he never used his powers to gain wealth. He was an honourable man. I belong to you now, and I will belong to your son and his sons, and their sons. Just obey my rules. Oh, and one last thing, be sure not to tell anyone about your gift. Humans are treacherous." Kuru says, his words echoing through my mind. I go to bed, my mind filled with thoughts of riches, things will soon change for the better.

The next morning, I shed a tear as grandpa's body wrapped in white cloth is lowered into the dirt. The ceremony is a quick one at Regent Community Cemetery.

Tamba En D Kofo (Tamba and The Vanishing Spirit)

Grandpa did not know many people, so his funeral is poorly attended. After the funeral, Peter joins me, and we head to Donald. According to Peter, he has a new job for us. At Donald's, we learn that there is a new location for us to raid later at night. We depart and plan to meet with John later in the day. I only have to do this three more times, and I can put all this behind me and go to school.

Later that night, John takes us inside Derrick Drive at Spur Road. The road is long, and un-tarred, the tires of the bike bump against the large stones littered across the drive. We jolt up and down on the bike but grip the cold metal bars of the bike tightly. I tap John on the back, signalling him to slow down and park by a curve in the road. "John, switch off the lights," I say to him, not wanting the single beam from his round headlight to draw attention to us. John nods in understanding and turns it off. He switches off the engine next. The night is perfect, with the moon hiding behind a cloud. Silence prevails though interrupted by the low humming of generators in the residences around.

Peter and I move stealthily along the path. We soon reach the house that is our target tonight. The walls of the house are very high, made of smooth brown marble tile. At the very top electric wires go right round the fence. There is a sign on it that reads, "Cross at your peril, fence well electrocuted." Peter lets out a low whistle and rubs his head in confusion. The gate is black, with gold designs, there is no way in. "How do we scale this? We cannot climb it, nor can we force the gate open." Peter says to me. I do not say a word and stay calm. I place my palm to the wall, and say *"Kofo, Kofo, Kofo."* My hand goes through, followed by my body.

Tamba En D Kofo (Tamba and The Vanishing Spirit)

I am inside the well-lit compound, flowers and trees line the fence. I can see a guard from a private security company, Ziral, patrolling the compound. I crouch down in the flowers and study his movements. I time him as he turns his back from the main house. I quickly sneak behind the house and hide. The main house is cream coloured and seems to be two stories tall.

From what Donald said, the Lebanese owners should be away for two weeks at their private Tokeh Beach resort. I place my hand to the wall, and say "*Kofo, Kofo, Kofo.*" I enter the dark room. I am on a mission, I put on the flashlight from my phone and move towards the door. Opening it, I pay no attention to the creaking sound of the hinges, soon I am in a hallway. I walk through the house, up the stairs, till I arrive at the second floor. I search for the master bedroom until I find it, I enter by placing my hand on the wall, I flash my light across until it lands on a picture of a chubby Lebanese man and his family of three. I let out a sigh of recognition. It is Ali Shaban, the owner of a popular gym at Wilkinson Road. I lift the picture carefully off the wall. Behind it is a grey, metal safe, inbuilt into the wall.

Donald is always spot on with his information. I wonder how he does it. I do not need to crack the lock of the safe. I just put my hand through it thanks to my newfound power. I feel around until my fingers grasp bundles of cash. I place them in my pockets, and hang the picture on the wall. I turn to leave, but it is crooked, so I readjust it properly. I retrace my steps, head down the stairs, and leave. In my excitement, I forget the patrolling guard and come face to face with him. He is startled, I sprint across the compound, touch the wall and reappear on the other side. "Run! Peter! Run! Peter!" I say. We run as fast as our legs can carry us, I can hear the guard unlocking the gate, and the metal locks rattling. We hop on the *Okada*, and by the time the guard starts shouting, we speed away. A few miles later, we arrive at our hideout behind *Old School*. "You mind telling me what you did there? What [16]*juju* are you using?"

Peter asks. "Oh boy, relax, is it not money you want? I will make us money. The only thing is that I can only do this two more times. So just keep your mouth shut." I say. I feel like I can take on the world now. Nothing can stop me. "In fact, after tomorrow, let us forget about Donald. We do not need to pay him a commission. We will start keeping the money for ourselves." I continue saying. "After what I have seen you do today, I am with you." He says. Peter loves money. He will go wherever there is money. I stand by the concrete wall pleased with myself. College used to seem like a far fetched dream, and now it is very much within my grasp.

"How dare you, boys! Unappreciative morons! After everything I have done for you!" Donald screams at us. He is visibly mad and not fond of my decision to leave. But my mind is made up, grudgingly, he tosses bundles of money on the floor for us. Peter and I bend over, pick up the money, placing it in our pockets. We walk out, as Donald yells insults at our backs. I give John his cut and part ways with Peter. For the first time, we have no idea where we will rob next. There is a certain excitement in the unknown.

---

[16] Juju: Local term for fetish practices. (Voodoo)

Tamba En D Kofo (Tamba and The Vanishing Spirit)

Over the next few days, Peter and I strategise. During the day, we spy on wealthy houses in the neighbourhoods of Hill station and Spur Loop. We bribe gatemen and workers of affluent households. We do this until finally, we get information on two houses, where the owners are due to travel. We find out where they keep the riches. Then at night, with Peter standing guard and John waiting outside to get away, I move through the walls. By the end of the night, we have hit it big. Richer than we ever dreamed, Peter and I split the earnings, we give John a better cut than usual. We are all happy. I can finally give up this life. I now have enough for my college tuition for the next three years. My future is about to change. "Your three chances are up boy, you can still use your powers, just not to gain wealth anymore," Kuru speaks through my mind, I have not heard his voice in a while. I have forgotten that he is still inside me. I ignore him. I do not need my powers anymore.

"Here, take this little something," I say to Sister Binty as I press some money into her hands. She looks at me with a puzzled expression on her face. "Tamba! Where did you get this from?" She says to me. "Do not worry, I won the lottery," I say. My heart skips a beat at the lie. She still looks at me with a quizzical look, but finally smiles and hugs me. "Thank you! Thank you! God will bless you!" She says, squeezing her hands around me. I just smile and walk to my room. Things are surely looking up.

I kneel by my bed, and draw out my cash box, I empty my pockets and arrange all the notes in it neatly. When done, I lie and decide that I will be heading to the college the next morning to make the necessary tuition arrangements. I lay with my hands behind my

64

head and shut my eyes. Sleep will come gently. Wherever grandpa is, I know he will be proud of me. Something cold rubs against my forehead, I swat it away drowsily and try to sleep again. The cold thing hits me in the middle of my head. I wake up frantically and leap out of bed. Fear grips me. I am staring into the barrel of a pistol. The wielder is a man, with a familiar lean frame, dressed in all black. The moonlight illuminates the room with a single straight beam. I make out two figures, the holder of the gun, and another masked man dressed in all black. The second man has his arms tightly around Sister Binty.

Fear renders her silent, her mouth tightly covered by the man's hand. "My friend, I know you have money here, take it out now!" The fellow says with a rough yet familiar voice. I refuse, without a word, he fires a shot at the ceiling. The loud bang sends a chill through my body, some debris from above drops to the floor, Sister Binty whimpers and trembles more violently. I sigh, the game is up. With shaking hands, I kneel, draw out my box, open it, and show the fellow holding the gun. He reaches out and grabs it with his left hand, his right hand still aiming the gun at me. I glance at his outstretched hand and spot a green spider-web tattoo on his lower left hand. "Peter!" I yell out, astonished. Peter does not say a word, but I know it is him. Too stunned to move, I watch as the man holding Sister Binty tosses her aside, and runs out with Peter. I cannot bring myself to look at Sister Binty in the eye. I just lay on the floor at a loss for words.

Broken, and in a state of despair, I go to the only place I have known as my haven. I walk past the wall, not in the mood to use my powers anymore. I enter grandpa's room. It is still as I remember, nothing untouched. I run my hands along his bed and sit by his pillow. I bring the pillow to my face, the familiar scent of grandpa still lingers on it. Something drops from it to the bed. It is a tiny yellow note. I pick it up, recognising grandpa's untidy penmanship immediately. "My dear Tamba, if you are reading this note, then I know you are in trouble. I am sorry I placed the burden of the *Kofo* on you. I have watched you struggle all these years to go to college, and I understand your pain. I just want to say I am proud of you. Check under the bed to find my last gift to you. Signed, your friend grandpa." I finish reading the note out loud. My thoughts churn, not quite comprehending what is going on. "What did grandpa leave?" I ask myself out loud.

With my heart beating against my chest, and my breathing accelerating, I kneel and check under grandpa's bed. I reach my hand around and feel a plastic bulge in the corner. I draw it out and wonder why it feels so heavy. I untie the knot securing it, letting out a sharp gasp, there is plenty of money in it! How did grandpa get this? I know he said someone owed him money some time ago, but I had no idea it was this much! "So does this mean I can go to college now?" I ask myself. I would not have to do anything illegal from now on. "Grandpa, grandpa, grandpa," I say out loud. He is always taking care of me. I leave the money under the bed, head for the door, and reach for the handle, but change my mind. Placing my hand on the wall next to it, I call out "*Kofo, Kofo, Kofo*."

CHAPTER 12

Di Witch Gun (The Bewitched Gun)

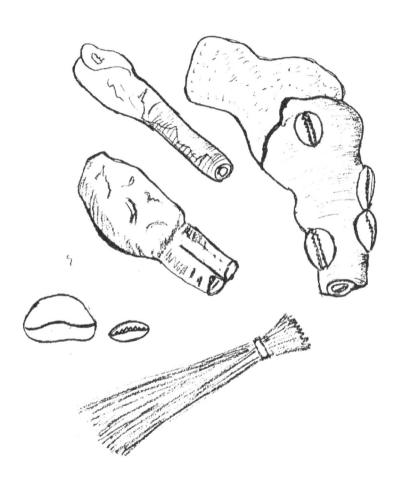

Di Witch Gun (The Bewitched Gun)

Starry night, grey clouds cover the moon
Crickets chirp and the trees wave in a gentle motion

The harmattan breeze blows with a whistle
The cloth cover to the hut dances in the wind

The cowries on his mat dance up and down
He draws them closer to the fire

The orange flames crackle and leap high
He welcomes the warmth, holds his hand up momentarily

Trying to catch the heat on his pale albino skin
The witch will be here soon

He moulds the tube, wrapping a red cloth around it over and over
again
Next, he takes the cowries, stringing them around the tube

He mutters some incantations, in the old language
His eyes roll upwards as the spirit of his ancestors flows through
him

He drops crystals of brown sugar in a large metal spoon
After the sugar, he adds snakeskin, black herbs, and scales from a
Mami Wata

The mixture bubbles and hisses as the metal glows red while the
flames lick it

Di Witch Gun (The Bewitched Gun)

He waits until the mixture is a thick yellow liquid

He pours this liquid into an oval, thin metal chamber
He allows the metal to cool, he utters one more incantation

The bullet will be invisible to the naked eye
He continues this process until he has ten more bullets

He proceeds cautiously to load them into the cowry covered tube
The *witch gun* is ready, and his client will be happy

A shrill whistle disrupts the nighttime silence, a dark hooded figure
peers around his entrance
She parks her broom by the side of his hut

She pays him three beating child hearts for his job
He smiles as he watches her fly away on her broom with her *witch
gun*

He feels sorry for the poor souls that will get hit with his bullets
They will know unimaginable pain and torture before they die

CHAPTER 13

Mahmood En Di Mami Wata (Mahmood and The Mer-maid)

The city shimmered under the moonlight. Streaks of silver reflected on the blue buildings. The buildings were peculiar. Each was tall, narrow, and bright blue. Rows of seaweed danced from side to side, in synchrony with the gentle current. The narrow paved streets were empty tonight. Every time I was down here, I never saw anyone. The blue city was always quiet, like a ghost city. Soon I heard it, a familiar song, a beautiful voice calling to me. My legs moved forward gingerly, not of my own accord. It serenaded and rendered me powerless. I just moved, enchanted by the enticing rhythm. I followed it until I stopped in front of a building with a bright red door. I placed my hand on the door, desperate to push it open. I was anxious to meet the owner of the voice. The door budged with creaking hinges, and I stepped in carefully.

"Cock-a-doodle-do" The call of a hungry rooster rang through the morning air, disrupting the serenity of people's sleep. I tossed and turned, burying my face in a pillow, and got up angrily. It had been the same dream for weeks now. I always woke up just as I was about to enter the red door. The question of what lay behind the red door plagued my mind often at night. I pushed these thoughts to the back of my mind. Today I had a daunting task ahead. Rolling off my mattress, I looked around my tiny room. There was a stove in one corner, a bag of rice leaned against the wall. Four pairs of shoes were arranged next to the radio, neatly on the floor. I slipped my foot into black, worn-out flip-flops, shoved a toothbrush into my mouth, and poured water from an orange gallon into a blue bucket. I then went outside to the [17]*wash-yard.*

---

[17] Wash-Yard: local bathroom, without a shower or bath tub, and usually accompanied by a latrine or bucket

The weather in Bonthe was always different from other places. Today it was windy, so windy, the dust from the side of the road rose
and intertwined with the air. I squinted my eyes, inhaling the
breeze, and continued walking. I went past the clock tower and
stopped outside a small, brown building. There were crowds of
people outside, yelling at the top of their voice. It was always like
this during elections. Even in a small coastal town like this, elections were still a big deal. Everyone wanted a slice of the political
pie. Some people wore purple, and others wore brown. There were
a small number dressed in grey. People only cared about two political parties in Bonthe. The National Alliance Party, and The Pro-
gressive Prosperous People's Party. The NAP had a group of hands
intertwined around a broom as its logo, and its supporters wore
purple. The PPPP had two lions holding a shield as its logo, and its
supporters wore brown. The NAP was more popular among the
east and west tribesmen of Sierra Leone, while the PPPP was more
popular among the southerners and northerners.

I weaved through the crowd and barged my way inside the city
council building. I straightened my grey shirt and walked confi-
dently to the stage, with my head held high. I was the front runner
for the Better Future For All Party. BFFAP was a new emerging
party birthed from the genius of Adam Smart. He was a doctor who
had returned from the United States and decided that it was time
for a better future in Sierra Leone. He preached against nepotism,
corruption, and sycophancy. His charismatic slogans, and powers
of persuasion, were slowly turning around the tides of the political
ocean in Sierra Leone. These were waters that were very tricky to
navigate, but the grassroots had bought into some of his ideas, and
he was proving to be a problematic malignant tumour in the organs

that made up the NAP and PPPP. So when Dr. Smart had come to the tiny coastal town of Bonthe, I had quit my job as a local journalist and signed up for his party. My fiery spirit and quick tongue had left a great impression on Dr. Smart. So much so that now I Mahmood was contesting for the position of mayor of Bonthe District.

I took my seat on the stage, flanked by the candidates of the other parties. Today was manifesto day, and the election would be held a week from now. The NAP candidate Musa Conteh went first. Musa was tall and smartly dressed. He spoke eloquently. He promised the people better light, better roads, the usual lies that politicians tell their supporters. Just before today, Musa had painted a few school buildings and installed a new water well for the people of Bonthe. So it was no surprise after talking, that he got a decent round of applause from the crowd. Next was the PPPP candidate, Sallu Komeh. Komeh had amassed a reasonable amount of wealth for a man in such a small town. He was the present mayor. He was a jolly short fellow, with a protruding belly filled with failed promises. As mayor, he had done nothing for Bonthe for the past four years. Yet he stood at the podium today in all his obese glory, asking for another term.

He had the money, he had the thugs, and more importantly, before today, the town had been receiving non-stop electricity. He even went for a jog a few days ago with some youth from the village. It was quite a picture to behold. After a few minutes, the man had collapsed by the side of the road. Nevertheless, today he stood at the podium, promising the people sweet nothings. They cheered for him with thunderous applause. It was the game of politics, and people were quick to forget. It was no doubt the reason why nothing ever changed. The people never demanded more of their leaders and were more easily waylaid by honey-laced promises and cheap gifts. Next, it was my turn. I approached the stage sure of my self. I spoke softly at first, reminding the people of our problems. Reminding them how long it took a transformer to get repaired, and that despite being famed for our fish sales, we still had nothing to show for it. I reminded them of how we had heard these same promises in the previous election. Yet, our children were still in the street trading for petty cash.

By the time I finished talking, everywhere was silent at first. Then the clapping started, softly at first, then it erupted into loud cheers and chants. It was to the heart of the everyday man that I spoke to, the man that had to toil all day in the farm for meagre earnings, while a politician rode by in the latest Prado jeep. The reception was more than I expected. I made my way outside to chants of "Mahmood! Mahmood!" Everyone wanted to touch me. From the corner of my eyes, I could see that Mayor Komeh was not pleased. He gave me a disgusting look before climbing into his jeep. The other opposition candidate Musa came over to congratulate me before getting into his vehicle. It was almost dark now. I pondered over how the election would be interesting as I walked home.

My house was a room in a compound of other tiny houses. We all shared one *wash-yard*. I was almost at my door when I felt a hand covering my mouth. A bag slipped over my head, and I felt myself lifted on to someone's shoulder. "Mayor Komeh would be happy with us. We will get rid of this foolish rat." A gruff voice said. His statement was met with hums of approval, as I felt myself tossed into the back boot of a car. I was worried and prayed over and over again. If only I had bodyguards like the other politicians, things like this wouldn't happen. The car bumped and rattled over the rough terrain. I kept hitting my head on the roof of the boot. Suddenly the car came to a stop. I heard the boot open and felt myself lifted once more. I felt My feet bound with something heavy. I was in panic mode. Before I could comprehend what was happening, I heard a splash. I felt water seep through my clothes, and I choked and coughed, twisting and fighting. It was no use. The last thing I remembered before my world went dark was a fall that never ended.

I woke up in a blue room and turned around, puzzled. Moonlight filtered in through tiny windows. Was I dead? I moved out of the room. The house I was in was very narrow. I had to turn sideways to move through it. Outside was like nothing I had seen. A blue underwater city, like the city I saw in my dreams every night. Unlike my dreams, it was not empty and quiet. It was alive, humans moved about, floating, some drove strange cars. Others seemed to be in conversation with fish. Taking a second glance, I noticed that these beings weren't normal humans. They had a single long fish-tail where their legs should be. Their tails shimmered under the light, each tail different from the other. My mind couldn't take any more of this. The whole scene left me flabbergasted. Then I heard it, the familiar song, the sweet, eerie voice. It called to me, and I went towards it. I stood in front of the red door in my dreams. Maybe this was just a dream. I never made it beyond this point.

I pushed open the door, expecting to wake up in my mattress. Instead, I was in a room that looked like a throne room of sorts. On a golden chair sat the most beautiful woman I had ever seen. She sang softly while playing a strange instrument. She beckoned to me with her hands. Her tail was large and pure silver. It draped on the floor, flapping up and down periodically. Her body was brown and shiny, like mahogany. A crown of colourful seashells adorned her head. I was in awe, and I moved closer, her voice pulling me in. "Hello Mahmood, I am Kasila." She said. Even her speech was smooth and sounded like a song. My heart stopped at the mention of her name. Everyone from Bonthe and the rest of Sierra Leone had heard of Kasila. She was a powerful marine spirit. According to stories, every year-end, she commanded great storms and capsized the boats of fisher-men. She claimed a vast number of lives every year. According to legend, she could grow to a great height and see the entire world from her view. If this was Kasila, and if I was really in her city, then there was no hope for me. I was definitely dead.

"Mahmood, fear not, you are my guest here. I have been watching you for a while now. About two months ago, I saw you by the waterside and took a liking to you. No harm will come to you. I want to help you." She said. "How can you help me?" I asked. "You should be dead right now if not for me. I brought you from the brink of death when you drowned. You impress me. With my help, you will win this election." She said. I stared back in shock, wondering how she knew all this. "If you help me, what do you get in return?" I asked. "I want you to be my companion. That's all I want. Just be my companion for two nights a week." She said. I was still in doubt. So all I had to do was be her companion, and I could win an election. If faced with this choice a few weeks back, I definitely would have refused. Now, it was different. The other politicians weren't playing fairly. I shouldn't either, as long as when I won, I did my duty to the people, how I achieved victory wouldn't matter.

"Ok, we have a deal. I will be your companion," I said. "Mahmood, darling, you have made the perfect choice. Keep in mind that I am a jealous being. I would not like to share you with anyone else when I visit on the nights I choose. You would not like to find out what would happen if you disobeyed me either." She said. Her face was dark as she said this. I did not pay it any mind. All I thought about was returning home and winning the election. I spent the rest of the night with Kasila. She showed me around her city. I learned that she could communicate with aquatic life and control the elements of nature to some extent.

The next morning, I woke up in my mattress. I was no longer in the underwater city. My conversation with Kasila still played in my mind. I rolled off and sat down for a moment to think about my next moves. Something brown caught my eye. It was a large [18]*calabash*. It wobbled precariously from side to side, next to my radio. I moved over to inspect further. I uncovered the wet layer protecting it, and my eyes opened wide in surprise. Bundles of cash filled it to the brim. It was definitely from Kasila. I was the voice of the people, and now I had the funds to give that voice some base.

The following days that led to the election, I ran a campaign like never before seen in Bonthe. I moved out of my shabby dwelling

---

[18] Calabash - a brown locally made bowl, usually used for cooking and holding different condiments.

and rented a two-bedroom apartment in the centre of town. I hired three bodyguards and bought a second-hand jeep. Every morning I gave the town youths a little money, and they would march around with my posters. I gave out money to market women and promised them a new market place that would accommodate them all. The chants of "Mahmood for mayor!" sounded in every corner of Bonthe. Every day, no matter how much money I took from the *calabash*, it always automatically replenished the next day. True to her word, Kasila visited me a day before the election. Her next scheduled visit was to be a day after the results would be announced.

On the day of the election, everyone was casting their ballots in the city council building, when a black jeep appeared, and thugs armed with machetes entered. They planned to intimidate the people into voting a party that was not their choice. The whole occurrence reeked of Mayor Komeh. I had expected this, however, and came prepared. Before the thugs could do any damage, they faced resistance by local boys that I had armed myself. One did not win an election without playing dirty. So the entire election proceeded calmly. At night, election officials counted the ballots. For the first time, an election went through successfully with no hindrance.

The next morning, with sixty percent of the votes, the Better Future For All Party had won. I was now mayor. Since it was a weekend, I would start work on Monday. For now, we had to celebrate. The celebrations carried on for two days. The people had gained freedom from the clutches of the parties that always won. It was history in the making. I vowed to myself not to be like the typical politician, and not to forget my roots. All too often, politicians entered office and lost their senses. They would forget friends, and humble beginnings, only to regain their humility and sense of self when their term ended. They forget that everything eventually comes to an end.

It was a day after the announcement of the election results. There was still a large party taking place at the city council building. I had been drinking more than usual. I never drink, but now I was mayor, I could do as I pleased. Everyone answered to me. As with all men when drunk, the senses dull, and all inhibitions fade away. It was the same in my case. After a few pints of star beer, I got to talking with an attractive female teacher. It did not take much for me to convince her to accompany the new mayor home. I was the top dog now. After a short drive, we arrived at my apartment. Still, in a drunken haze, I fumbled with the keys in the lock. Finally, I managed to open it and led her to my room. My new room was more spacious than my last, and I now had an actual bed instead of just a mattress on the floor. The best part was it had a bathroom self-contained, no more trips to the *wash-yard*. So I left my companion sitting at the edge of my bed and ran to the bathroom to ease myself.

I came out refreshed and ready to entertain my guest. I let out a yell. She lay on the bed, stiff and unmoving. I rushed over, frantically feeling for a pulse, but to no avail. "You disobeyed me, Mahmood. Did I not give you everything?" Kasila's voice sounded through the room. I could not see her. I had forgotten she was supposed to visit tonight. Before I could react, I felt a sharp headache, and I blacked out. I woke up in Kasila's throne room. She had a dark, fearful expression on her face. Then she smiled a sweet smile. "You did not listen to me. You can never return to the surface world again. You belong to me forever. My slave for eternity." She said with an evil smirk.

On Monday, things unfolded in this way: the new mayor did not show up to work. Upon further investigation, his body was discovered, alongside that of a female teacher, in his new apartment. The new mayor, a former journalist, had shown up out of the blue. Overnight he had grown ten times rich and had won an election while contesting under a relatively unknown party. His death, and that of his female companion, just added to the theories that people had formed. The most popular opinion was that he sacrificed a human to win the election, but the devil had come to collect, and things had backfired. It was not uncommon for African politicians to get accused of rituals. The political wheel waited for no man. Mayor Komeh had placed second in the election, and he was sworn in swiftly for a second term. Greed, sycophancy, nepotism, these were the pillars on which politicians perched. Politics was a dangerous game. Only a few played it and won.

As for me I had bitten more than I could chew. I had to live with the consequences of my decisions. I looked around my new world, stared up at the fish swimming in a straight line, and walked towards the red door.

CHAPTER 14

Di Salone Uman (The Sierra Leonean Woman)

19

_____

[19] The poem "Di Salone Uman" won first place in the First Nations Poetry Magazine, Canada: Poets Of The First Nations Contest. (Di salone uman illustration was done by Mariatu Saccoh)

81

Di Salone Uman (The Sierra Leonean Woman)

Let me weave a tale

A tale of elegance and magnificence

A tale of beings so out of this world

Their mere presence moulded the earth

From the tip of the Nile to the jungles of the Madagascar

Their grace shone like the river Congo under the burning sun

Their curves could only be compared to the palm tree swaying

Swaying In the gentle breeze of the Atlantic Ocean

O yes these creatures were gems

It was said that their smile

Deserved a place on the peak of pyramids

It was said that their eyes

Could bring water to the Sahara

These Queens these Empresses

Dragged in chains but still

Still they glowed

Rise they shall again

Have you ever seen a lioness?

You don't need to see one

To hear her roar

You don't need to see a A Sierra Leonean Queen

To hear her cry

It is said that the sun sets

As a way of bowing down to her highness

There is good and evil in everything. Just because one possesses the knowledge of how to do evil does not mean they will use that power.

Printed in Great Britain
by Amazon